An Amish Christmas Surprise

By
Ruth Bawell

Table of Contents

Unsolicited Testimonials

By **Phyllis**

⭐ Love Ruth!

I love Ruth's books! Her mysteries are the best!

⭐ Love This Author

Ruth Bawell is very creative and a great writer! All her books have left me unable to stop reading till the ending! There were a few Amish fact mistakes, like unmarried man having a beard, but the plot was so good I overlooked that!

By **Steve M**

⭐ I love romance stories August 5, 2017

I love romance stories... well written with her usual twists to the story still enjoyed them very much Once I start I can't put it down.

By **Bones**

⭐ Amish County Stories

I love all the Amish County stories! Each one brings so much excitement! Ruth Bawell is also a wonderful writer!

By **Kindle Customer**

⭐ Good clean writing.

The Amish stories of Ruth Bawell are authentic, faith-filled writings. They are short, more the length of novellas or longer short stories. Always clean, always uplifting.

FREE GIFT

Just to say thanks for checking our works we like to gift you

Our Exclusive Never Before Released Books

100% FREE!

Please GO TO

http://cleanromancepublishing.com/gift

And get your FREE gift

Thanks for being such a wonderful client.

CHAPTER ONE

"*Gute mariye,* Miss Faith," Miriam Shrock greeted her neighbor, Faith Miller. "Please come inside. It's really cold today, isn't it?" She stepped back as Faith walked inside, huddling into her shawl, and glanced out as she shut the door. "Would you look at all that snow!" Miriam exclaimed.

"*Gute mariye* to you too, my dear Miriam," Faith replied. "*Wie bischt du?*"

"I'm very well, Miss Faith," Miriam answered. "But I miss my *mamm* and *daed* and all my younger siblings." She sighed. "Especially as it's Christmas time and school is closed, so I don't have a lot else to do aside from my chores."

"Oh, my dear child, that's why I'm here. I've brought you some of your favorite chocolate muffins from the bakery."

"Oh my!" Miriam exclaimed. "I'll make us some hot chocolate, in that case."

As Miriam handed Faith a steaming mug of hot chocolate, she noticed the older woman wincing as she hooked her fingers around the handle of the mug.

"What's wrong, Miss Faith?" Miriam asked.

"My arthritis is acting up, as it usually does in this weather," Faith replied with a shrug.

"There's not much I can do, except keep my hands as warm as I can. But it's painful, and is hampering my work in the bakery." She took a sip from her mug and then looked at Miriam over the rim. "I feel like the time may have come to shut down Faith's Bakehouse," she declared.

"What? No! You can't do that, Miss Faith!" Miriam protested. "Your bakery is an institution that Pinewood Gap can't do without."

"I can't keep going like this, Miriam," Faith said sadly. "It's a struggle every day, and I can't trust just anyone with the baking." She sniffed at the air, suddenly distracted. "What's that heavenly fragrance?" she asked.

Miriam smiled shyly at Faith. "I've just been experimenting with blueberry cinnamon buns, and took a batch out of the oven a few minutes before you knocked on the door."

"Well then, my dear, what are you waiting for?" Faith said. "Fetch us some of those divine buns—unless you're saving them for someone else—and let's eat them with this delicious cocoa you've made."

Miriam jumped up happily and went off to fetch the buns.

"These buns are perfect, Miriam," Faith said. "You are a very talented baker, you know."

"Thank you, Miss Faith," Miriam replied. "Coming from you, that's high praise indeed."

Faith's eyes narrowed momentarily and then widened as a thought struck her. She hit her forehead with the flat of her hand and clicked her tongue. "How foolish I am," she said. "All this while the answer has been right in front of me, and I haven't seen it."

"What answer, Miss Faith?" Miriam queried, looking confused.

"You, my child. You! You are the answer to my dilemma. Miriam, would you consider taking a job at our bakery? Please, my dear? Just for the Christmas season, so I don't have to close down and disappoint all our regular customers?"

"But Miss Faith," Miriam began, "Your legendary confectionary requires somebody with both skill and experience, and I have…"

"You, my dear Miriam, have what it takes. I will be there training you. I promise, I won't be too strict an employer, and the pay will be good," Faith smiled.

"In that case," Miriam said, "when do I begin?"

The next day, Miriam followed Faith into her bakery. It was a charming place, with white lace curtains at the windows and red and green tablecloths on the tables to mark the Christmas season.

"Miss Faith," Miriam said, sniffing the air appreciatively, "just the aroma in here makes me feel like I've come home."

"Well, that's what all our customers say, which is one of the main reasons that I've kept the place going despite not always feeling like I'm up to it," Faith replied.

"I'm here to help any way I can," Miriam said.

"Could you start by making a batch of those delicious blueberry cinnamon buns?" Faith asked. "They will be much appreciated."

"You actually want to feature them in your store?" Miriam asked, her jaw dropping.

"Of course," Faith replied. "They are perfect. I hope you don't mind my using your personal recipe."

"Mind?" Miriam said, wide-eyed. "I am so honored, Miss Faith!"

"Come on then, my dear, and let's get to work," Faith said. "We have to make some gingerbread men as well today, and a whole range of Christmas cookies."

"Miss Faith, do you mean you do all this by yourself?" Miriam asked, incredulous.

"I do," Faith answered. "And believe me, it's helped me get through many a day when I could otherwise have felt lonely and miserable. Having people swarm through that door, keeping my hands busy and my heart full, has helped me forget that I could never have children." She stopped. "Forgive me, Miriam, I didn't mean to lay all this on you." She smiled. "You know, I'm so glad we've been neighbors all these many years, and Micah and I are so grateful that you all always had us over on Christmas."

"That's because you both have been like family to us, Miss Faith," Miriam replied with a happy smile.

CHAPTER TWO

The snow was coming down so hard that Adam Lapp could barely see a few feet in front of him. This was definitely not the most ideal weather in which to be driving around in a buggy. Adam wished he had just stayed home rather than choose that particular day to visit Pinewood Gap's famous bakery to stock up on Christmas confectionery. When his horse began to balk, Adam knew he would have to stop and wait for the snowstorm to pass. But it only got worse, and eventually, Adam unhitched the horse, climbed on, and decided to find his way to Faith's Bakehouse on horseback.

"There's a man riding up on a horse," Miriam said, looking out of the window through the flurries of snow.

"It can't be an Englischer," Faith remarked, going back into the kitchen. "So it must be someone from our village who has had to abandon his buggy."

Miriam rushed over to the front door as Adam stopped just outside. "You may take your horse to the stable at the back and then come in!" she called out cheerily.

Adam huddled into his coat and hurried back to the bakery after stabling his horse. He summoned a smile as Miriam threw open the front door for him and stepped aside to let him enter. He looked at the young girl with her blue gown and white *kaap*, hazel eyes and a radiant smile and returned her greeting.

"*Guder nummidaag*," he said, shaking the snow off his hat.

"Welcome to Faith's Bakehouse," Miriam said. "Come in from the cold and warm up with a mug of hot chocolate while I take your order." She looked past him and out of the door he had just come through.

"Oh my!" she exclaimed. "Did you actually *choose* to ride in this weather?"

"No," Adam replied. "I drove here in my buggy, which I had to abandon some way from here because the wheels just refused to move after a while."

"And your horse brought you here," the girl said, her eyes wide with wonder.

"It was tough going," Adam remarked. "But at least I got here."

"I'm Miriam Shrock," the girl introduced herself.

"I'm Adam Lapp," Adam replied. "And I've come all the way from Green Wood village to stock up on your Christmas confectionery. The fame of Faith's Bakehouse has spread to our village as well.

"We have some of the finest blueberry cinnamon buns, fresh out of the oven," Faith announced, breezing in. "Miriam here has made them herself using her signature recipe."

As Miriam blushed, Adam's eyes fell on the tray of buns that Faith had placed on the counter. "I'll take two dozen please," he said.

"You must have a very large family to feed," Miriam remarked, as Adam went down the array of baked goods and added more items to his order.

Adam shook his head, and his mouth briefly went down at the corners. "No," he replied. "Actually, I don't have any family to feed. I live alone. I lost both my parents a couple of years ago, and I have no siblings. I buy this confectionery to share with my neighbors, but also to enjoy by the fireside in the evening when I'm alone."

Faith gave him a sympathetic look. "I'm sorry to hear that," she said.

"How about a blueberry cinnamon bun with a mug of hot chocolate while you wait out the snowstorm," Miriam suggested.

"Thank you," Adam replied. "I would welcome something warm to drink, because I can virtually feel the snow in my bones." He looked eagerly at a table set by the fireplace. "Could I sit down there?" he asked.

"Of course," Faith said. "And grab the table fast, because I can see more customers trudging through the snow and heading this way!"

Adam settled into the large, upholstered chair, the only one of its kind in the store. Miriam soon arrived with a cinnamon bun and a mug of steaming hot chocolate and set them down on the table in front of him.

"This chair is so comfortable," Adam said, leaning back.

"Well, I'm glad it is," Faith said, joining them, "because it looks like you're going to be here a good long while, judging by the looks of that snowstorm outside."

"Where's your buggy, Adam?" Miriam asked.

"Roughly a thirty-minute horse ride away from here," Adam replied. "And I suppose we'll have to dig it out of the snow when I go to retrieve it.”

“Micah, my husband, will help you when the storm lets up,” Faith said.

Sometime later, Faith came out of the kitchen and stood by the window.

“The storm hasn’t let up,” she observed. “How do you intend getting back to Green Wood, Adam?”

“I suppose I’ll have to go in search of somewhere to spend the night,” Adam replied. “Is there an Inn close by?”

“None that I would advise you to try and find in this storm,” Faith replied.

“In that case, I have no idea what I will do,” Adam replied. “Maybe the snow will stop in a little while,” he added hopefully.

“You can stay the night at our home,” Faith said suddenly.

Adam looked at her in surprise and shook his head. “I couldn’t possibly impose on you like that,” he replied.

“I would much rather that you stayed with me, and I knew you were safe, than that you set off in that storm, leaving me wondering if you were alright,” Faith declared.

"I am touched that you would even worry about my welfare when we have only just met," Adam said.

"That's Miss Faith," Miriam laughed. "Her heart is big enough to accommodate every customer that walks through these doors."

"And here I thought I was being given special treatment," Adam joked.

Faith and Miriam echoed his laughter, and the atmosphere was as warm as the fire that crackled in the hearth.

"Well, I don't think I've ever invited my customers to stay over at my home so far," Faith said, "so yes, Adam, you are being given special treatment."

"In that case," Adam said, "I am happy to accept your offer."

***

"You will fit nicely into one of my suits," Micah said, showing Adam to their spare bedroom.

"You and Miss Faith are very kind," Adam replied gratefully. "Thank you so much."

"Miriam is here, Micah!" Faith called out, and Micah turned to Adam.

"It's time for supper, son. Wash up and join us in the kitchen."

"I live next door," Miriam said, in response to Adam's curious look when he saw her bustling around the kitchen. "And Miss Faith has been kind enough to offer to keep an eye on me while my parents and siblings are away visiting my grandparents."

"It's a treat for us to have Miriam here, and for us to keep popping into her house next door," Faith declared. "She's like the daughter we couldn't have, and Micah and I love her like our own."

"Stick around long enough, and you'll be accorded the same privilege," Miriam said, smiling across the table at Adam.

Adam looked downcast for just a fleeting moment; then, he rapidly regained his composure and nodded his head. "I look forward to that," he said, "because I really do miss having family, most especially at this time when everybody has someone to spend Christmas with." He looked embarrassed. "Oh dear, there I go feeling sorry for myself."

"It's normal at this time of year," Miriam said sympathetically.

"Yes," Faith chimed in. "Feel free to share your feelings. We're here to listen, because we've all felt lonely at some point."

"But right now," Micah said, "we all have each other. So let's thank the Good Lord for our food and eat, because I'm hungry!"

Adam managed a chuckle. "I'm hungry, too," he said. "And you're right. I have company on a night when I anticipated being completely alone, eating more baked goods than are good for me!"

"Well, now you get to eat more baked goods than are good for you, except that you have company doing it!" Faith laughed.

Miriam was quiet, looking at the faces around her in the lamplight and feeling a sense of gratitude that she lived right next door to Faith and Micah.

"Please let me help with your evening chores," Adam said to Micah as the ladies cleared the table and began washing dishes.

"I would be grateful for your assistance," Micah replied.

"We used to have more cows," Micah explained to Adam as they entered the dairy shed. "but we had to give them up because it was becoming more and more difficult to take care of them. Now we just have these two beauties who provide enough milk for our needs. My wife has been suffering from arthritis and is unable to do too much nowadays. However, she is brave and courageous and carries on with her chores to the extent that she can do them."

"The fame of her bakehouse has spread far," Adam replied. "So I hope she doesn't have to give that up."

"Baking is her passion," Micah remarked. "But she feels the time has come to pull the shutters down on Faith's Bakehouse once for all. This Christmas might be the last one when she will be selling her baked goods." He sighed. "Thank God for Miriam, who stepped in to help out. She's a wonder, is that girl. Can do anything she puts her mind to."

"You and your wife seem so fond of her," Adam said. "And she of you. One would almost think you were of the same family."

"The Shrocks are like family to us," Micah replied. "Which is why they felt comfortable enough to leave Miriam here alone to take care of their house and animals while they were away. They knew we would look out for her. But mostly, I suspect, they left her here so that she could look out for us."

"It's stories like these that give meaning to the Christmas season," Adam said, nodding sagely.

"You're a good lad, Adam Lapp," Micah said, patting him on the back. "And if the snow stops tomorrow, I'll go with you to find your buggy."

The snow didn't ease up until two days later, and in that time, Adam Lapp found himself feeling more and more at home with Faith and Micah Miller… and Miriam Shrock.

"Adam!" Miriam called out as he and Micah brought his buggy round to the front of the Miller's home. "Tell me when to load the food into your buggy!"

Adam smiled. "My buggy is almost ready," he called back.

"Thank you for all the work you put in to get my buggy in working order," Adam said gratefully to Micah.

Micah adjusted his hat on his head and looked up at the sky. "You had best hurry back if you don't want to get stuck in another storm," he laughed.

He patted Adam on the back. "It's been wonderful getting to know you, Adam," he said. "And thank you for letting me work on your buggy. It feels good to know I haven't lost my touch!"

"I wouldn't have been able to get those wheels on if you hadn't been there," Adam laughed. "Someday, perhaps I could come by, and you could teach me how you do that?"

Micah nodded and smiled. "It would be my pleasure," he said.

"Adam!" Faith said, coming quickly down the porch steps. "Please come back and visit us. I need to know that you're safe and doing alright."

"Of course," Adam said. "I will, Miss Faith."

"Here," Faith said, handing Adam a large knitted sweater. "You keep that and wear it, ok?" She blinked rapidly as she spoke, and Adam was moved.

"I will, Miss Faith," he replied. "And thank you for your hospitality and most especially for this sweater."

He looked up as Miriam came towards them, staggering under the weight of a pile of boxes. "The baked goods," she said breathlessly.

"Oh, I would've come in and fetched them myself," Adam said, rushing forward to relieve Miriam of her load.

"I'll go back and get the ham and pies," Miriam said.

"Ham and pies?" Adam queried.

"Just a little food that Miriam and I cooked for you," Faith murmured. "Just so that you would have something nice on a cold evening."

"I have no words," Adam whispered, feeling a lump in his throat.

He followed Miriam into the kitchen and looked at the large leg of ham and the array of pies that lay there, ready to be loaded into his buggy.

"That's a lot of food," he said. "How would I eat all that by myself?"

"Miss Faith and I thought that it might be nice if you invited your neighbors over when you get back. So you wouldn't feel quite so alone, you know."

"Miriam," Adam said, "I am moved beyond anything that you all would think of how I would feel going back, and then cook all this food so that I could have people over to help me feel less lonely."

"And please do come back to visit," Miriam said. "Because it would mean a lot to Miss Faith and Mister Micah. They have been so happy having you stay these past days."

"I will definitely visit," Adam assured her.

CHAPTER THREE

Faith set the piping bag down and painfully flexed her fingers.

"It's hard when a task that I love becomes hard for me to perform," she sighed.

Miriam brought her a bowl of warm water and sprinkled some herbs into it.

"Soak your hands in this for a while, Miss Faith," she said. "And leave the piping to me."

"But there are so many Christmas cookies to decorate and all those cake orders to finish as well," Faith said.

"Perhaps we should hire another hand?" Miriam suggested.

"Could I apply for the position?" a voice said from the doorway.

"Adam!" Faith and Miriam chorused.

"Miss Faith! Miriam!" Adam greeted them. "It's so good to see you both!"

"Just seeing you fills my heart with more joy than you would know," Faith declared. "Thank you for coming back to visit!"

"I couldn't stop thinking of Pinewood Gap and Faith's Bakehouse," Adam said. "So I had to drop by. But I will only stay the day if you let me help you."

"Oh, you dear boy," Faith crooned. "It does my heart good to see you."

"And of course you may help," Miriam chimed in. "I'm willing to give you a crash course in decorating Christmas cookies."

"Actually," Adam said, taking his hat off and rolling up his sleeves, "I used to assist my *mamm* in the kitchen at Christmas time, so I learned how to decorate cookies and even cakes. But I would like to take your crash course all the same."

"You can decorate cookies?" Miriam queried, her eyes wide with mingled delight and disbelief.

Adam picked up a cookie. "Let me demonstrate my skills, and if I pass the test, then you must let me help out," he said.

Miriam and Faith watched as quickly and expertly Adam added colorful piping to the snowflake-shaped cookie.

"Oh my!" Miriam exclaimed, when Adam showed her his handiwork, "you are actually very good!"

"So good that I wish we could hire you for the Christmas season. I believe my fingers are getting stiffer and more painful each day," Faith added.

"You know," Adam said, "I'm not exactly doing a lot back home, so maybe I could come by every day and help out."

"You would do that?" Miriam asked, incredulous.

"I would," Adam replied, decorating cookies with speed and dexterity.

"If you keep going like that, you're going to give me a complex," Miriam remarked with a chuckle.

"You and Miss Faith are the ones with all the talent, actually baking these cookies and cakes. I'm only good at decorating them because we always used to have a Christmas Cookie Decorating Contest which my mamm organized at Green Wood. She insisted that I participate with all the others in our village, and made sure I had enough practice to do a decent enough job."

"It sounds like a lovely event to have during the Holidays," Miriam remarked. "And it encourages everyone to participate."

"It certainly fostered a sense of community, because all the cookies were donated to a foster home or an orphanage," Adam said.

"Do you still host the event?" Miriam asked.

"Not since *Mamm*...." Adam began, but didn't complete the sentence.

"I'm sorry," Miriam said.

"Maybe, Miriam, we could all go to Green Wood Village to visit Adam. And we could help him host the Christmas Cookie decorating contest," Faith suggested.

"You would do that for me?" Adam whispered, emotion making it difficult for him to speak.

"Just as you would consider coming over every day to help us with the work at the store," Faith replied.

"I do believe there's a reason why my buggy broke down in the snow," Adam declared.

"Miss Faith," Miriam said, as they walked back home from the bakery, "that was a very lovely idea to go to Green Wood and help Adam host the cookie decorating contest. You really have begun to care about him a lot, haven't you?"

"Indeed I have," Faith admitted. "Though we have only known him for a short time. I suppose the fact that he doesn't have his parents anymore, and the fact that Micah and I don't have children, somehow makes me think that what he says is right. There was a reason why his buggy broke down in the snow that day.”

“I think so too, Miss Faith,” Miriam said.

“There he is now, helping Micah shovel the snow in the driveway,” Faith said as they rounded a corner.

“And I thought he had started back for Green Wood,” Miriam said.

“He did say that he wanted to stop by and return Micah’s sweater, so I suppose he did just that, and is shoveling snow now!” Faith replied.

Miriam chuckled as she turned into the Shrocks’ front yard.

“I will see you for supper, dear,” Faith called out to her.

“Yes, thank you, Miss Faith,” Miriam called back.

As she walked up her porch steps, she turned to look over at the Millers’ house. It was right next to her own, and she saw Adam waving out to her. She waved back and called out a greeting to Micah. However, walking through her front door made her realize that she missed her family, and she wondered how Adam lived without one every day of the year.

“I’m so fortunate,” Miriam said aloud to herself. “That I have my *mamm* and *daed* and siblings, and Miss Faith and Mister Micah as well."

She was going about her evening chores, cleaning out the cow byre after feeding the chickens, when Adam came in.

"Miss Faith wanted me to check on you," he said.

"She worries too much, does Miss Faith," Miriam laughed. "But it never ceases to amaze me just how much she cares."

"May I help you?" Adam asked.

"You've been helping us all so much, Adam," Miriam said seriously. "What will we all do if you should suddenly stop coming by?"

"Why would I stop?" Adam queried, giving her an equally serious look.

"I don't know why I said that," Miriam replied, feeling a bit foolish. "But I just did."

"I like helping out," Adam said, filling a water trough. "It gives me a sense of belonging."

"I suppose I understand," Miriam said. "I feel the same way when my family is away and I'm over at Miss Faith's house. Helping in the kitchen makes me feel like a member of her household."

"I had a lovely time shoveling snow with Mister Micah," Adam remarked. "He always gives me good advice, like my *daed* would do. It's a wonderful feeling." He sighed. "Well, I should soon be heading back to Green Wood. I have an early start to drive back here tomorrow."

"It must be tiring driving your buggy back and forth," Miriam remarked. "But I suppose you have to get home to do all your chores."

"I don't have a lot of chores to do," Adam said. "I gave up the chickens and cows, so I just have my buggy horse to take care of."

"How do you… umm… make a living?" Miriam asked.

"I hire myself out during harvest time, which is why I'm free during the winter. I build houses for a living too, and put my hand to almost anything."

"So, why do you need to get back home every day?" Miriam asked, and then wondered if there was a way she could retract her question.

"I have to return because that's the place where I live," Adam replied.

"Yes, of course," Miriam said. "I should have asked why you continue to live in Green Wood, if you have so little to keep you there."

"Until that fateful day when I broke down in the snow," Adam said, "I only ever knew life in Green Wood. It was thanks to you, Miss Faith and

Mister Micah that I discovered the possibility of life elsewhere.”

“Does that mean you are considering relocating?” Miriam asked curiously.

“I’m not sure,” Adam said, “but the thought has crossed my mind.”

“Miss Faith will be overjoyed, I’m sure, and Mister Micah will no doubt suggest different ideas for employment,” Miriam responded with a smile.

“And you?” Adam asked. “I mean,” he said hurriedly, “what would you say if I were to consider such a life-changing move?”

“I would say you should do whatever makes you feel complete,” Miriam replied.

“You are very wise for one so young,” Adam remarked.

“I’m eighteen, so I suppose I’m not so very young at all,” Miriam countered with a laugh.

“I am twenty-five years old,” Adam declared. “So, I suppose in comparison to me, you are very young… but also very wise for your age.”

“Thank you for the compliment,” Miriam said. “I accept it with gratitude, as I accept your help with my chores.”

As they walked back to the house, Adam lowered his voice. “Please don’t mention that I’m considering relocating to Pinewood Gap to Miss Faith or Mister Micah," he said. "Not until I make a decision."

"I'm glad you also feel that we shouldn't tell Miss Faith or Mister Micah anything until you actually are ready to make the move," Miriam replied.

Later, as they sat down to supper, Adam looked across at Miriam and gave her a secretive smile. Miriam returned it and then felt a gentle, indefinable warmth slip over her like the lightest of winter shawls. It felt good to be sharing a secret that would make Faith and Micah's faces light up like a thousand lamps when it was revealed.

CHAPTER FOUR

"I hope these cookies are enough for the decorating contest in Green Wood," Miriam said as she pulled the last few trays of Christmas cookies out of the oven.

"Well, they had better be enough," Faith replied, "because we have to get them into boxes now and be prepared to leave very early tomorrow morning for Green Wood Village." She winced as she attempted to carry one of the trays of cookies, and Miriam hurriedly took it from her.

"Miss Faith, you need to soak your fingers in warm water infused with herbs at least five times a day during winter," she said.

"But there's not a lot of time to do it in between meeting all the Holiday orders," Faith replied.

"I'm sure Adam would be happy to help out with all the extra work, Miss Faith, or we could hire somebody until Christmas Eve," Miriam said. "You just need to sit in the store and tell us what to do."

Faith sighed. "It's not just the store I'm worried about, Miriam. Micah and I aren't getting any younger, and at this stage in our lives, it would be nice just to have a young pair of hands to help us out a little," she said.

"And that's what I'm here for, Miss Faith," Miriam replied. "As well as *Mamm, Daed* and my younger sister and brothers."

"What would we do without you all?" Faith said, giving Miriam a hug.

"What's that in the oven?" Faith asked, looking over Miriam's shoulder as she hugged her back.

"Some roast veal and a couple of pies," Miriam answered. "For Adam." She shrugged. "I thought it would be nice for us to take him some food... so that he doesn't need to scurry about figuring out what to cook for us."

***

Adam was watching the children in his kitchen filling piping bags with colored frosting when he heard buggy wheels approaching. He ran to the window and looked out, and a memory returned for a brief moment. It was of buggy wheels in the driveway and guests alighting to participate in the cookie frosting competition. It was such a long-awaited event, because, at the end, everyone joined in to take the frosted cookies to the homeless, singing Christmas Carols along the way.

As he looked out of the window, he saw Miriam step down from the buggy, followed by Faith. He ran outside just as Micah parked the buggy and jumped down.

"I can't believe you all are here!" Adam said. "And I am overjoyed that you are!"

But as he guided his friends into his home, his spirits failed him.

"You seem very quiet, Adam," Faith remarked. "Is everything alright?"

"This is going to be more difficult than I anticipated," Adam replied, holding back a sigh.

"How so?" Miriam queried.

"Because I haven't told you the whole story about the Christmas Cookie Decorating Competition that we held each year," Adam said.

"Please tell us, Adam," Micah urged.

"My *mamm* had a bakery just like you have, Miss Faith," Adam began. "It was because I missed her so much that I traveled to Pinewood Gap to find similar confectionary. One of the people in our village had told us about Faith's Bakehouse."

"Oh Adam," Faith whispered. "I am so sorry. I never should have suggested that we revive this event."

Adam looked away. "This whole competition was my *mamm's* idea to get the village together, to serve the ones less fortunate as a Community. But the last time we hosted this event..." Adam said haltingly, "something tragic happened."

There was silence as Faith, Micah and Miriam moved closer to hear what Adam was about to reveal.

"We were all in our buggies, returning from a round of carol singing, having successfully distributed frosted Christmas cookies and warm clothes to the homeless, when we got caught in a snowstorm. It was very dark. None of the buggies had anything but lanterns hanging on the front. The buggy that my parents were in went rolling down a slope and collided with a tree." He cleared his throat. "That's why this is going to be hard for me. I thought it would be alright, but I suppose I will need more time to be able to forget that horrific episode which stole them from me."

Miriam and Faith had tears flowing down their faces.

"I'm so very sorry, Adam," Miriam whispered.

"And so am I sorry, son," Faith said.

"Adam," Micah spoke shakily. "I haven't discussed this with my wife, but I am sure she will agree with me when I ask if you will consider coming to stay with us for the rest of this season. We never realized just how hard it must be for you."

"It is," Adam replied gruffly, "far harder than I revealed to you. And I would like nothing better than to come and spend the holidays with you all. Life here, despite our wonderful neighbors, is too filled with memories of my parents, and seeing them everywhere… in everything… is just too difficult during Christmas."

"We can set off for home right away if you would like to," Micah said.

"No," Adam replied resolutely. "I will not let a moment of faintheartedness on my part deprive both the residents of Green Wood and the homeless people outside our village of a wonderful event planned just for them."

"That's the spirit, my boy," Micah said. "Do this for your *mamm* and *daed* to keep their memory alive."

Later, on the way back to Pinewood Gap, Miriam leaned back and closed her eyes. She was feeling immensely grateful that though her family was away, at least she had the assurance that they were returning soon, unlike Adam, who had to face the fact every day that he was alone in the world.

"Are you asleep?" Faith asked.

"No, Miss Faith," Miriam replied, opening her eyes. "I was just thinking about Adam's story and feeling really sad that he has to be so alone in the world."

"I know," Faith said. "I keep complaining that Micah and I don't have children, while Adam has nobody."

"I'm really glad you asked Adam to come for Christmas, Mister Micah," Miriam remarked. "And it obviously cheered him up immensely because he conducted the competition with such joy and enthusiasm."

"It was a labor of love," Faith said.

"The children were so lovely," Miriam mused. "And so talented." She chuckled. "And the winners were so thrilled with their prizes!"

"I liked how every child who participated got a prize," Faith said.

"And I think it was wonderful how all the women of Green Wood Village baked pies for the prizes," Miriam replied.

"I enjoyed singing Christmas Carols and distributing all the beautifully frosted cookies to the homeless," Faith sighed. "Did you notice all those bright, happy smiles of appreciation? I think we should do something similar in Pinewood Gap."

"And we can ask Adam to organize it," Micah suggested.

"That's an excellent idea, Mister Micah," Miriam said enthusiastically. "You have had the best ideas today!"

"He certainly has," Faith agreed with a smile.

CHAPTER FIVE

Miriam looked out of the window and smiled to herself. Adam was outside, shoveling snow with Micah. They chatted as they worked, and looked so happy. She smiled again as she saw Faith come outside with mugs of steaming hot cocoa. The feeling of happiness remained with her as she went about her chores, and she realized, with a sense of wonder, that she was happy because Faith and Micah were happy. "Could my happiness be tied up in the joy of another?" Miriam mused.

Later, chores done, she went off to work at Faith's Bakehouse, but saw, to her surprise, that the shutters were down.

"Miss Faith!" she called out, going around to the back door to see if it was open. "Miss Faith!"

"Miriam!" she heard Adam call. "Miss Faith said to tell you she is sorry, but she will be late today."

"Oh!" Miriam exclaimed, worried. "Is she alright?"

"She is in a bit of pain," Adam said, "so she requested me to come in to help while she takes some time to soak her fingers in warm water and herbs as you suggested."

"Oh, I am glad she's getting the opportunity to do that," Miriam replied.

"She has offered me a job here over the holidays," Adam said. "And I accepted to help her out."

"You are very kind," Miriam remarked. "And Miss Faith could certainly do with some time to look after herself and get some well-earned rest."

"Well," Adam said, "here I am, ready to do whatever you need me to."

"I'll get started on cleaning out the store and getting the fruitcakes into the oven," Miriam said.

"I'm good at mixing batter," Adam announced. "Along with my cookie decorating skills, that's another thing I learned from helping my *mamm* at our bakery.

"I think it's a wonderful coincidence that your *mamm* also ran a bakery," Miriam remarked as she swept the floors and dusted the tables.

"I think so too," Adam replied. "But the most wonderful thing for me was to be invited to spend Christmas here with two people I have grown to love and respect."

"Miss Faith and Mister Micah are truly kind and caring," Miriam said.

"And they think the same of you," Adam declared.

"Really?" Miriam replied, glowing with pleasure at the compliment.

"So do I, actually," Adam added.

"Oh… you are making me feel very self-conscious and embarrassed now," Miriam protested.

"I have never met people who are so ready to accept me into their lives," Adam declared, "until now."

"I think you met the ones that truly needed you in their lives, Adam," Miriam remarked sagely. "And I do believe that God arranged for you to meet them."

"But I have to return to my home, I suppose, when the holidays are over," Adam sighed.

"You don't have to, Adam," Miriam said. "You could always look for work here while you decide whether you want to move here permanently or not. You also have a job here at Faith's Bakehouse, but maybe you'd be glad for something you might enjoy more, like farm or construction work."

"Yes, that's a good suggestion," Adam said. "I can't bear the thought of returning to our empty house."

"I'm sorry about… what happened," Miriam murmured. "I haven't been able to stop thinking of it and what it must have been like for you."

"It was two Christmases ago," Adam said. "And I have been struggling to come to terms with it for all this while." He paused as he gathered his thoughts. "It was coming here that really improved things for me," he said. "I actually felt happy for the first time since I lost my family, because I had inadvertently stumbled upon another." He shook his head. "Not that I can ever forget my parents. But at least I can go on with life now in a more positive manner."

"I'm so happy with the way things worked out for us all," Miriam said, smiling at Adam. She realized in that moment that he had lovely eyes— and a very nice smile. As if with a new realization, he returned her look, and Miriam caught her breath and quickly looked away.

"I'd better get down to mixing the fruitcakes," she said, setting the broom and mop aside. "People will start coming in for hot cocoa and other goodies, and I will have to wait on them."

"Let me help," Adam said, picking up the large mixing spoon and basin.

Miriam was already weighing out the ingredients. "You can start creaming the butter and sugar together," she said.

"I'm glad we, as a Community, still use non-mechanized ways to do things," Adam remarked.

Miriam sighed. "Well, I suppose we preserve the authenticity of the art of baking by following the process the old-fashioned way, but I sometimes wish we were allowed to use some appliances." She smiled. "But that's only an idle thought and not a heartfelt desire. My desire is just to be able to own a store like this one. I think Faith's Bakehouse is the most amazing store in all of Pinewood Gap."

"It is," Adam agreed.

"What was your *mamm's* bakery called?" Miriam asked.

"Lapp's," Adam replied.

"Did you ever want to keep it going?" Miriam queried.

"I did try," Adam replied, furiously creaming butter and sugar in the mixing basin. "But it was far too painful going in every day and having to employ someone to do what my *mamm* had done by herself for so many years. So I shut it down."

"I can't even begin to imagine how that must have been for you," Miriam remarked.

"I feel better now that I can talk about it," Adam said. He smiled. "So you want to have your own bakery?"

Miriam blushed. "No," she said. "It's just a dream—to own a store like this one. But to be honest, I am happy just being employed by Miss Faith."

"Will you go back to teaching?" Adam asked.

Miriam shook her head. "I would have loved to," she sighed. "I enjoyed the job, but now someone younger will take over from me. I was contemplating requesting an extension of my services. But ever since I started working here, I think I'm happy to do this forever!"

"I think Miss Faith is happy to have you here forever," Adam remarked. "She can't stop talking about how talented you are… and how helpful."

"You're making me feel self-conscious again," Miriam warned him with a laugh. She cracked some eggs into a bowl and mixed them into the creamed butter and sugar that Adam had been whipping furiously.

"It's time for the fruit," Miriam said, sprinkling handfuls of dried fruit over the batter. Adam folded them in with practiced skill, and Miriam couldn't help being overcome by a sense of joy at how well they were working together.

When the customers came in, Adam left Miriam to tend to the ovens and went out to wait on them. Miriam was amazed at how it seemed as if he had always been there at the counter of Faith's Bakehouse, or in the kitchen mixing cake batter.

Soon after a group of Englischer tourists came and went, there was a lull.

"You must be hungry," Miriam said to Adam. "As am I."

"I guess there is some leftover pie for us," Adam replied.

"Actually, I made some stew this morning and brought it along with me to share with Miss Faith. Since she isn't here…"

"I'd love some," Adam said eagerly.

"And I've baked some fresh herb bread as well," Miriam added.

She set a bowl of steaming hot stew before Adam, with a plate of buttered herb bread.

"Aren't you going to eat something too?" Adam asked.

"We can't leave the counter unattended, so we'll take turns to have lunch," Miriam replied. She was thinking all the while that having a meal alone with Adam might raise eyebrows in Pinewood Gap, even if it was a working lunch.

"I'm sorry," Adam said, coming out to where Miriam was standing by the counter.

"What for?" Miriam queried.

"This must be awkward for you having me here in the store," Adam replied.

"On the contrary, you are such a big help," Miriam said. "And I'm glad that Miss Faith is getting some well-earned rest."

"Or maybe she has had enough rest," Adam chuckled, pointing out of the window.

Miriam looked out and laughed, glad that she wasn't going to be left alone with Adam for the rest of the afternoon. She didn't want things to become awkward between them, and she guessed that he was already sensing her growing discomfort.

"How did you both fare without me?" Faith asked as she stepped into the bakery.

"We missed you, Miss Faith," Miriam replied. "But I think we managed not to mix up orders… and I have finished a batch of fruitcakes."

"You have slipped so effortlessly into the routine of the bakery, Miriam," Faith said. "And I am so happy to see that you and Adam have been able to handle things on your own today. It gives me hope that even if I decide to give up the business, there will be somebody to take it over."

"Faith's Bakehouse cannot function without you, Miss Faith," Miriam said firmly. "So please don't think of giving it up so quickly. When winter has passed, your arthritis won't be quite so difficult to deal with, and then we can bake together again."

"Miriam," Faith said, "I hope you will consider making Faith's Bakehouse yours permanently. You fit right in as if this place has been waiting for you to walk in and make it your own. Think about it, dear."

"I wouldn't be able to afford to buy it, Miss Faith," Miriam said. "It would take me a lifetime to raise the money, even if I wanted to make this beautiful store my own."

"It's not money I want," Faith said. "The only thing I want is to hand the bakery over to someone who would run it like I would."

"I couldn't just take it from you, Miss Faith," Miriam said.

"Miriam, please think about it," Faith pleaded earnestly.

"Right now, you're here, Miss Faith, and I am here to help you run the bakery," Miriam said gently. "Anyway," she continued, "we have to concentrate on Pinewood Gap's version of The Christmas Cookie Decoration Competition, and we need to get a tent organized to cover the area outside the bakery."

"I'll take care of the tent," Adam chimed in. "And we should do something that we always did in Green Wood. Apart from all the children participating, we could get the families to compete against each other to frost the most cookies in a given amount of time."

"That sounds like a lot of fun," Miriam remarked.

"It is," Adam replied. "At Green Wood, it brought families together. It enabled them to have fun and reinforced their sense of loyalty to each other."

"To think of the impact that a simple competition makes," Faith remarked. "Your *mamm's* idea was wonderful."

"It spread good cheer amongst the homeless and just gave everyone a sense of belonging," Adam said. He rubbed his hands together. "I am going to organize the tent now," he said, striding away purposefully.

"This event has already stirred up quite a lot of excitement amongst our Community here in Pinewood Gap," Miriam remarked, "and I can't wait to get the children together and teach them some piping tricks before we get started."

"I can see that you're missing your job at the school already," Faith said. "Children are a gift, Miriam, and now it's time you stopped caring for other people's children and had some of your own."

Miriam chuckled. "Miss Faith, I would have to get married first… and before that, I would have to be courted, and before that, I would have to meet somebody who is interested in courting me," she declared.

"Who knows, child, that person may be closer than you think, and you may meet him around the next corner," Faith replied.

Miriam smiled and shook her head, then turned to check the dough rising on the counter.

"Oops!" Miriam said, almost colliding with Adam as he re-entered the bakery.

He stopped and stared at Miriam for one long moment. "I'm sorry," he murmured, suddenly awkward.

Miriam gave him a quizzical look, wondering what had changed between the time he had gone outdoors to organize the tent and the time he returned.

"Did you manage to find a tent, Adam?" Miriam asked. "Mister Micah said that he knew where we could hire one or two, depending on our need."

"Yes, I'm going to meet someone called Dan Troyer. He's going to help us get a tent. I came back here because I left my hat behind in my hurry to be off," Adam answered, looking away to the side and not directly at Miriam.

"Adam," Miriam queried, "are you alright? You look a little pale."

"*Ik ben oke,*" Adam answered gruffly, picking up his hat and hurrying away.

"The event will be wonderful, Adam!" Miriam called after him, anxious to reassure him.

Adam turned around briefly to nod at her, and then leapt into his buggy.

"I think Adam is nervous about how the cookie frosting competition will go here in

Pinewood Gap," Miriam murmured to Faith, as she rolled out a fresh batch of cookie dough a few days later. "He has suddenly become awkward around me, and I hardly ever see him now."

Faith smiled at Miriam. "Miriam, my child, I know you have never been courted, and that even your Rumspringa was relatively uneventful because you chose not to go ahead with more than a week of it. But surely your intuition should tell you why Adam has suddenly become awkward around you." She lowered her voice. "I saw Adam about to enter the door as we were talking, and then he drew back, and was possibly listening to our conversation," she said.

"Oh my!" Miriam exclaimed. "Did he hear you say that the person interested in courting me may be around the next corner? And does he think…?"

Faith chuckled. "I don't really know, but I suppose it must have got him thinking… because you bumped into him on the way out, didn't you?" She chuckled again. "And he must surely have begun to realize that the Good Lord certainly had a plan when He brought him here."

"The Good Lord's plan was for Adam to be of assistance to you and Mister Micah and to have a home and two wonderful people to spend Christmas with," Miriam replied.

"And maybe to find the right partner to spend his life with?" Faith said. "He is a very personable young man, with a good heart too. He is everything that a young woman would desire in a husband."

"Miss Faith, Adam is so much older than I am. He is twenty-five!" Miriam remarked.

"My dear child," Faith said with a sigh, "that is the perfect age difference. The Lord knows that it's always good to marry a man who is mature and can take care of you."

"But Miss Faith," Miriam said, "I am not ready to be married!"

"You are, Miriam," Faith declared. "You just don't know it yet. Allow yourself a little time to think about Adam and see him for who he truly is. Unless, of course, you have already been considering his many attributes?"

Miriam blushed. "Miss Faith, Adam is not only older than me, but wiser. I doubt he even notices me… in that way. He is always so serious and preoccupied," she said.

"He has been through one of life's worst tragedies, Miriam," Faith replied. "Please give him a chance to open up to you. All I ask is that you

think about what God must surely have planned
when He brought Adam here."

CHAPTER SIX

Miriam walked home deep in thought. Faith's words had stirred up a frenzy of conflicting emotions within her. As she trudged through the snow, the breeze blew her *kaap* off, and she bent over to retrieve it. As she straightened up, she saw Adam's buggy coming towards her. She moved to the side, still holding her *kaap* in her hand.

"The tent is up, and everything is ready for the cookie frosting contest," Adam said, pulling up. Miriam nodded, suddenly tongue-tied. She felt awkward because she had her *kaap* in her hand and her hair was uncoiling itself, tossed by the chilly breeze.

"I'd best be on my way," Miriam said, wishing the ground would open and swallow her up. Suddenly she and Adam couldn't even talk to each other anymore, and it was distressing. "Just when I thought I had a friend," Miriam murmured to herself as she walked hastily away, pulling her *kaap* firmly over her locks as she did so.

"Please wait!" Adam said, jumping down from his buggy and running after her. "I must speak with you."

"What about?" Miriam asked, turning around and facing Adam, her lips trembling ever so slightly for no apparent reason.

"Have I upset you, Miriam?" Adam asked.

"Only because we once used to talk to each other with such ease, and now I appear to have done something to make you change your attitude towards me," Miriam replied.

"You haven't done anything wrong, Miriam," Adam said. "I have just been very confused."

"Well, that makes two of us, Adam," Miriam replied. "Because I am confused too. Why would you suddenly behave so strangely towards me? You don't even come around to the store anymore, lest you run into me, I suppose."

"I have offered to buy the store from Miss Faith," Adam said.

"And is that making you behave awkwardly around me?" Miriam asked.

"I want to ask if you would manage the store because I know nothing about the business," Adam continued, ignoring Miriam's question.

"If you don't know anything about the business, then why are you buying the store?" Miriam asked.

"Because… it's… where I met you, Miriam," Adam said, turning red. He took off his hat and began to twirl it nervously.

"I don't quite understand," Miriam said, her voice almost inaudible as the wind began to howl.

"I want to court you," Adam blurted out. "You are the most beautiful, kind girl I have ever met, and I don't think I could stand to be away from you. I'm moving to Pinewood Gap."

Adam paused for breath, biting down on his lower lip and looking at Miriam uncertainly as she stared at him wide-eyed.

"Please, Miriam, all I ask is that you think about it," Adam said.

"This has all happened so suddenly," Miriam said, half to herself. "I need my *mamm* to explain it to me. I don't understand this at all," she added, and began to weep. She was embarrassed by her display of emotion, but she felt so overwhelmed and unsure.

"I can see that I've distressed you without intending to. I just had a moment of clarity when I knew exactly what I should do, and I did it. But I can see that I ought to have waited," Adam mumbled.

"You must ask my parents, but I must go now," Miriam said through her tears. "I'm sorry. I have a lot to think about."

She ran all the way back to her house, filled by the emotions that had welled up within her that she couldn't comprehend.

***

"Mister Micah," Adam said, as they shoveled snow together the next day, "I don't have any experience of… umm…women."

Micah smiled. "Are you going to ask me for advice regarding a certain young lady?" he queried amusedly.

Adam turned red as he nodded. "It must be quite obvious to you and Miss Faith," Adam said, "that I have begun to feel quite deeply for Miriam."

"And you don't know how to tell her?" Micah asked.

"I don't," Adam admitted. "I just came right out and told her I wanted to court her, and I revealed to her that I had offered to buy the store from Miss Faith… because…"

"Miriam is a capable young lady when it comes to teaching in school and managing the bakery, but when it comes to matters of the heart, she has little or no experience," Micah said. "Faith and I have known her since she was a little girl and we have watched her grow. She has always been more involved with her work at the school or at the bakery, or her chores at home, which makes her the perfect choice for a wife. If you want my advice, Adam, waste no time in telling this young lady exactly how you feel."

"She told me I must ask her parents," Adam replied. "About courting her, I mean."

"That's what I mean," Micah said, nodding approvingly. "She follows the rules, and that's what makes her such an asset to our Community. She has the greatest respect for her elders and such compassion."

"I suppose I don't deserve somebody like her," Adam murmured.

"She needs someone like you, Adam," Micah replied. "She needs someone older who will guide and advise her. You and Miriam complement each other perfectly, as Faith says."

"Miss Faith has spoken about us to you?" Adam asked, embarrassed.

"She has talked of nothing else for the past few weeks," Micah answered. "I do believe she has had many a conversation with God on the subject. You see, Faith thinks the world of you both, and there is nothing she would like better than to see you both together."

"Thank you, Mister Micah," Adam said. "I see things even more clearly now."

"That's good," Micah said. "Now hurry! We have a cookie contest to go to, and the event can't begin without you!"

"I'll fetch my buggy," Adam replied.

"Adam," Micah said, "you are just like a son to us. Having you here is the best gift that The Lord could give us this Christmas."

"You and Miss Faith are my Christmas gift, Mister Micah," Adam replied. He smiled. "I'm moving to Pinewood Gap for good. I have been looking for farm work, but in the meanwhile, my *daed* left me enough to invest in a small business like Miss Faith's store. I mean, if she would let me buy it for Miriam to run."

Micah smiled. "I can see you are thinking of the future, and that makes me very happy, but I don't think Faith intends on selling the store at all," he said.

"She isn't?" Adam queried. "Well, I'm sure Miriam will be happy because she enjoys working there with Miss Faith."

Micah gave Adam an enigmatic smile. "You worry about that cookie competition, Adam, my son, and let the rest be. God has a way of working things out, you know."

CHAPTER SEVEN

"I can't believe it's Christmas Eve already!" Miriam exclaimed as Faith walked into her kitchen shivering.

"And what a wonderful time we had yesterday at the Competition!" Faith remarked.

"Adam was right, too. It brought families and our Community together," Miriam replied, remembering the many glances they had exchanged as they worked together with the children.

"It was wonderful to participate as a family too," Faith mused. "You know, piping those designs on the cookies, I actually forgot my arthritis for a while and didn't even feel any pain!"

"It was one of the best Christmas events we have ever had in Pinewood Gap," Miriam agreed. "And next year, I hope I'll have …." She leaned out of the window. "Miss Faith! Could that be…? Is it….?"

"It is!" Faith said, and the two women left the window and ran to the front door.

"*Mamm*! *Daed*!" Miriam exclaimed. "You're home! Abel! Caleb! Mary!" She ran from one sibling to the other, hugging them, and then threw herself into her mother's arms.

"Your grandparents are better and insisted that we come back to celebrate Christmas with you. We wanted to bring them back with us, but they said they would travel here in warmer weather," Dorcas Shrock, Miriam's mother, explained.

"And we missed you too much," her father, Jeremiah, added.

"You're just in time. Miriam has been cooking and baking preparing Christmas Eve supper," Faith said.

***

Miriam set the candle holder on the table and stood back.

"My child," Dorcas remarked, "this meal looks so delicious!"

"There's someone we want you to meet," Micah said, coming in with Adam.

"This is Adam Lapp, and he has become like a son to us," Faith added.

Dorcas and Jeremiah greeted Adam, and Miriam introduced him to her siblings.

"Let us say a prayer of thanks for the food," Jeremiah said.

"Before that," Adam cut in, "I would like to say something."

"What is it, Adam?" Dorcas asked as Adam got to his feet.

"I'm not good with words," Adam began. "But I want to say thank you, to all of you, for making me feel like part of your family." He cleared his throat and glanced at Miriam. "Miriam, the other day, I asked you a question, and you told me I must ask your *mamm* and *daed*. Today, this is what I am going to do if that's alright with you."

Miriam blushed and nodded.

"Miss Dorcas and Mister Jeremiah, I just want to say that …"

"Just a minute, I have to interrupt," Faith cut in.

"Yes, Miss Faith?" Adam queried.

"I am gifting Faith's Bakehouse to you, Miriam, because I love you like a daughter… and because I know that you will run it like I have done all these years."

"Miss Faith!" Miriam exclaimed and began to protest, but Faith held up her hand. "No more on that subject, my child. The matter is settled," she declared firmly. "You may proceed now, Adam," she added.

Adam cleared his throat again. "I was going to buy the bakery for Miriam to run, because that is the place where I first met her—the girl whose hand I want to ask for in marriage." He turned to Faith. "And if you won't sell it to her, I hope you will sell it to me—for her," he winked.

Faith's grin broadened, and she gave a barely perceptible nod. "We'll discuss that later, young man. But I am very happy to see the Bakehouse will be in good hands."

"Marriage!" Miriam exclaimed, jumping to her feet. "I thought you said you wanted to court me!"

"Miss Dorcas, Mister Jeremiah," Adam said, "I want to court, and marry, your daughter Miriam. If she will have me."

"We haven't been away that long," Dorcas said, looking mystified, "and our daughter has grown up so much!"

"What do you say, *Mamm*? *Daed*?" Miriam asked hesitantly.

"What do you say, my child?" Jeremiah asked. "We have yet to get to know Adam. But it would seem that you have come to know him in the time that we have been away.

"I say yes," Miriam whispered.

"Then so do we," Jeremiah and Dorcas chorused.

"Well, Micah, we have a son and a daughter given to us this Christmas. What better gift could we have asked for?" Faith smiled.

The End

FREE GIFT

Just to say thanks for checking our works we like to gift you

Our Exclusive Never Before Released Books

100% FREE!

Please GO TO

http://cleanromancepublishing.com/gift

And get your FREE gift

Thanks for being such a wonderful client.

Please Check out My Other Works

By checking out the link below

http://cleanromancepublishing.com/rbauth

Thank You

Many thanks for taking the time to buy and read through this book.

It means lots to be supported by SPECIAL readers like YOU.

Hope you enjoyed the book; please support my writing by leaving an honest review to assist other readers.

.

With Regards,

Ruth Bawell